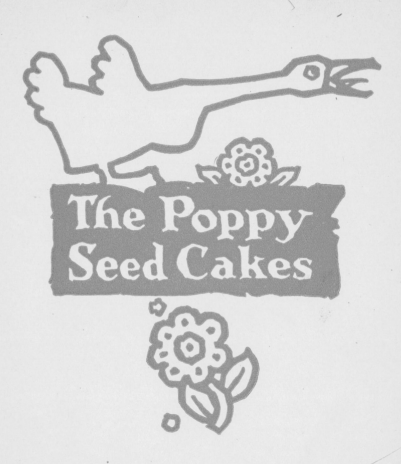

The Poppy Seed Cakes

AUNTIE KATUSHKA BROUGHT A HUGE BAG FILLED WITH PRESENTS

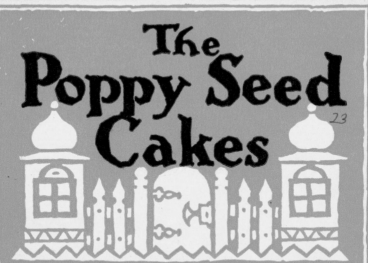

The Poppy Seed Cakes

By Margery Clark

Illustrated by
Maud & Miska Petersham

Garden City   New York
Doubleday, Doran & Company, Inc.
1936

THE POPPY SEED CAKES

ONCE upon a time there was a little boy and his name was Andrewshek. His mother and his father

brought him from the old country when he was a tiny baby.

Andrewshek had an Auntie Katushka and she came from the old country, too, on Andrewshek's fourth birthday.

Andrewshek's Auntie Katushka came on a large boat. She brought with her a huge bag filled with presents for Andrewshek and his father and his

mother. In the huge bag were a fine feather bed and a bright shawl and five pounds of poppy seeds.

The fine feather bed was made from the feathers of her old green goose at home. It was to keep Andrewshek warm when he took a nap.

The bright shawl was for Andrewshek's Auntie Katushka to wear when

AUNTIE KATUSHKA STARTING HOME FROM THE MARKET

she went to market.

The five pounds of poppy seeds were to sprinkle on little cakes which Andrewshek's Auntie Katushka made every Saturday for Andrewshek.

One lovely Saturday morning Andrewshek's Auntie Katushka took some butter and some sugar and some flour and some milk and seven eggs and she

rolled out some nice little cakes. Then she sprinkled each cake with some of the poppy seeds which she had brought from the old country.

While the nice little cakes were baking, she spread out the fine feather bed on top of the big bed, for Andrewshek to take his nap. Andrewshek did not like to take a nap.

SHE SPRINKLED EACH CAKE WITH POPPY SEEDS

Andrewshek loved to bounce up and down and up and down on his fine feather bed.

Andrewshek's Auntie Katushka took the nice little cakes out of the oven and put them on the table to cool; then she put on her bright shawl to go to market. "Andrewshek," she said, "please watch these cakes while you rest on your fine

feather bed.   Be sure that the kitten and the dog do not go near them."

"Yes, indeed!   I will watch the nice little cakes," said Andrewshek.   "And I will be sure that the kitten and the dog do not touch them."   But all Andrewshek really did was to bounce up and down and up and down on the fine feather bed.

"Andrewshek!" said Andrewshek's Auntie Katushka, "how can you watch the poppy seed cakes when all you do is to bounce up and down and up and down on the fine feather bed?" Then Andrewshek's Auntie Katushka, in her bright shawl, hurried off to market.

But Andrewshek kept bouncing up and down and up and down on the fine

feather bed and paid no attention to the little cakes sprinkled with poppy seeds.

Just as Andrewshek was bouncing up in the air for the ninth time, he heard a queer noise that sounded like "Hs-s-s-s-sss," at the front door of his house.

"Oh, what a queer noise!" cried Andrewshek. He jumped down off the fine feather bed and opened the front

BOUNCING UP IN THE AIR FOR THE NINTH TIME

door. There stood a great green goose as big as Andrewshek himself. The goose was very cross and was scolding as fast as he could. He was wagging his head and was opening and closing his long red beak.

"What do you want?" said Andrewshek. "What are you scolding about?"

"I want all the goose feathers from

your fine feather bed," quacked the big green goose. "They are mine."

"They are not yours," said Andrew-shek. "My Auntie Katushka brought them with her from the old country in a huge bag."

"They are mine," quacked the big green goose. He waddled over to the fine feather bed and tugged at it with

his long red beak.

"Stop, Green Goose!" said Andrew-shek, "and I will give you one of Auntie Katushka's poppy seed cakes."

"A poppy seed cake!" the green goose quacked in delight. "I love nice little poppy seed cakes! Give me one and you shall have your feather bed."

But one poppy seed cake could not

THE GREEN GOOSE TUGGED AT THE FINE FEATHER BED

satisfy the greedy green goose.

"Give me another!" Andrewshek gave the green goose another poppy seed cake.

"Give me another!" the big green goose hissed and frightened Andrewshek nearly out of his wits.

Andrewshek gave him another and and another and another till all the poppy

seed cakes were gone.

Just as the last poppy seed cake disappeared down the long neck of the green goose, Andrewshek's Auntie Katushka appeared at the door, in her bright shawl. "Boo! hoo!" cried Andrewshek. "See! that naughty green goose has eaten all the poppy seed cakes."

"What?   All my nice little poppy

seed cakes?" cried Andrewshe's Auntie
Katushka. "The naughty goose!"

The greedy goose tugged at the fine
feather bed again with his long red
beak and started to drag it to the door.
Andrewshek's Auntie Katushka ran after
the green goose and just then there was
a dreadful explosion. The greedy goose
who had stuffed himself with poppy seed

cakes had burst and his feathers flew all over the room.

"Well! well!" said Andrewshek's Auntie Katushka, as she gathered up the pieces of the big green goose. "We soon shall have two fine feather pillows for your fine feather bed."

THE WHITE GOAT

ONE fine Saturday morning Andrewshek's Auntie Katushka said, "Andrewshek, I must go to market and buy a goat."

Andrewshek was playing in the garden. He had pulled out some of the feathers from his fine feather bed and had put them in his hair. He looked very funny.

As Andrewshek's Auntie Katushka went out of the gate to go to market, Andrewshek said, "May I go with you, Auntie Katushka?"

"No, Andrewshek!" said his Auntie Katushka. "You must stay at home. Please watch to see that the dog does not open the gate and let the chickens and the cat run out into the road."

"Yes, indeed, I will watch to see that the dog does not open the gate. And I will be sure that the chickens and the cat do not run out into the road."

Then Auntie Katushka, in her bright shawl, hurried off to market. But all Andrewshek really did was to swing backward and forward and backward and forward on the dark green gate.

Andrewshek loved to swing backward and forward on the gate just as much as he loved to bounce up and down on his fine feather bed.

ALL ANDREWSHEK DID WAS TO SWING BACKWARD AND FORWARD
AND BACKWARD AND FORWARD

At the market Auntie Katushka saw a white goat. The white goat had a long beard and a short tail. "That is just the goat I want!" said Auntie Katushka.

"White Goat!" said Auntie Katushka. "I am going to take you home with me to Andrewshek."

"Who is Andrewshek?" said the goat.

"Andrewshek is a little boy who lives across the tracks and up the hill, in a little house with a dark green gate. Andrewshek loves to swing backward and forward and backward and forward on the dark green gate."

"I would not be surprised if Andrewshek was swinging backward and forward on the green gate now," said the

goat to herself. "I think I'll run ahead and see."

She galloped off.

"Stop, White Goat!" cried Auntie Katushka. "Stop!"

But the goat did not stop. She ran faster and faster, across the tracks and up the hill until she came to the little house with the dark green gate. Andrew-

shek was swinging backward and forward and backward and forward on the dark green gate. The chickens and the cat had long before run out into the road.

"How do you do, Andrewshek?" said the white goat.

"How do you do, White Goat?" said Andrewshek. "Where are you going?"

"HOW DO YOU DO, ANDREWSHEK?"

"No further!" said the white goat. "I belong to your Auntie Katushka."

"Where is my Auntie Katushka?" said Andrewshek.

"I ran away from her, across the tracks and up the hill; and here I am!" said the goat.

"Won't Auntie Katushka be surprised when she sees you here!" said Andrewshek.

"I think I will hide!" said the white goat.   She ran behind the little house.

Andrewshek's Auntie Katushka, in her bright shawl, came hurrying up the hill.

"Andrewshek, I bought a sweet white goat at the market, to give us milk for our poppy seed cakes.   She ran away and so we cannot have any poppy seed

cakes to-day. I wonder how we can
find her!"

"Ha! ha! ha!" the sweet white goat
called out. She had climbed to the top
of the roof where she could look down
on Andrewshek and Auntie Katushka.

"Come down from the roof, you
naughty White Goat!" said Auntie Katushka.

The goat shook her head.

"Please come down!" said Andrewshek. "And I will give you a big poppy seed cake."

"I do not like poppy seed cakes," said the naughty white goat.

"What shall we do?" said Andrewshek.

Andrewshek's Auntie Katushka

"I DO NOT LIKE POPPY SEED CAKES," SAID THE NAUGHTY WHITE GOAT

went into the house and took off her bright shawl.   She put on her apron.

She washed some turnips and some parsnips, two onions and four carrots for the soup.   Then she cut the green tops from the vegetables.   She put the green tops in a basket. "Goats love fresh green tops," she said to Andrewshek, as she put the basket on the back porch by

the door. She left the door wide open.

The naughty white goat was peeping over the roof to see what she could see. She saw the green tops in the basket by the kitchen door. Immediately she felt very hungry. She clambered down from the roof. She stole up to the basket.

"Well! well!" laughed Andrewshek's

Auntie Katushka, as she slipped a halter around the white goat's neck. "We soon shall have plenty of milk for our poppy seed cakes."

THE PICNIC BASKET

ONE cool summer morning Andrewshek's Auntie Katushka said, "Andrewshek, I think I will put some sandwiches and some cottage

cheese and some poppy seed cakes and two eggs in our picnic basket. Then we will go to the park and eat our lunch there, near the water."

"May I go with you, Auntie Katushka?" said Andrewshek.

"Of course you may go to the park with me," said Auntie Katushka. "But first we have a great many things to do,

before we can start to the park. I must
go into the garden and catch the white
goat. I will tie her up so she will not
run away. Please find the kitten, Andrewshek, and put her in the cellar, so
she will not worry the chickens while
we are gone."

"Yes, indeed, I will find the kitten
and put her in the cellar," said Andrew-

shek, "so she will not worry the chickens while we are gone."

But all Andrewshek really did was to lift up the red and white napkin which Auntie Katushka had laid over the picnic basket and look at the eggs and the poppy seed cakes and touch the sandwiches and taste the cottage cheese.

The goat was not easy to catch. The

THE GOAT WAS NOT EASY TO CATCH

goat wanted to go to the park, too.   She
galloped round and round the garden.

At last Auntie Katushka caught her
and tied her firmly to a post.

Then Auntie Katushka went into
the house to get Andrewshek and the
lunch basket. She saw Andrewshek
peeping under the red and white napkin
and tasting the cottage cheese.   He had

forgotten all about the kitten.

The kitten was nowhere to be found. "I think she must be paying a visit to the Mouse family," said Auntie Katushka.

Then Auntie Katushka put on her bright shawl and took her umbrella with the long crooked handle under one arm. Then she picked up the lunch basket with the red and white napkin on top and

she and Andrewshek started for the park.

They went down the hill and across the tracks and past the market and down a long street until they came to the park by the water.

Andrewshek sat down on the grass beside a little stream. Andrewshek's Auntie Katushka laid her umbrella with

ANDREWSHEK SAT DOWN ON THE GRASS

the long crooked handle and the basket
of lunch on the grass beside Andrewshek.

"Andrewshek," said Auntie Katushka, "I must go to the spring and get
some water for us to drink. Please
watch the basket with the eggs and the
sandwiches and poppy seed cakes and
cottage cheese while I am gone."

"Yes, indeed, I will watch the basket of lunch," said Andrewshek.

But what Andrewshek really did was to say to himself, "I would like to take off my shoes and my stockings and wade in the little stream. I believe I will!"

Andrewshek took off his shoes and his stockings and went wading in the little stream.

A big white swan came floating calmly down the stream. He saw the picnic basket lying on the grass. He stopped and stretched and stretched his long neck, till he could touch the basket. "Honk! honk! honk!" said he. "I wonder what is under the red and white napkin."

The big white swan lifted the napkin

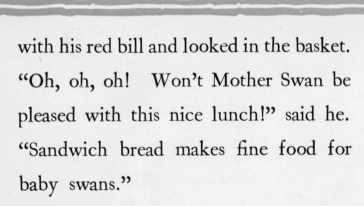

with his red bill and looked in the basket.
"Oh, oh, oh! Won't Mother Swan be
pleased with this nice lunch!" said he.
"Sandwich bread makes fine food for
baby swans."

He picked up the basket in his strong
red bill and floated it ahead of him down
the stream.

Andrewshek could not wade after

ANDREWSHEK COULD NOT WADE AFTER THE BIG WHITE SWAN

the big white swan.   The water was too
deep.

"Stop! stop! White Swan!" cried
Andrewshek.   "That is my Auntie Katushka's picnic basket and it has our
lunch in it.   Please put it back on the
grass."

"No, indeed!   I will not put the
basket back," honked the big white

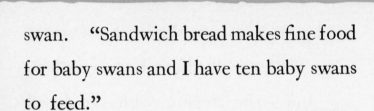

swan. "Sandwich bread makes fine food for baby swans and I have ten baby swans to feed."

The big white swan gave the picnic basket a little push with his red bill. The basket floated on down the little stream. The big white swan floated calmly behind it.

Just then Andrewshek's Auntie Katushka came hurrying up with the spring water. She saw the big white swan floating down the stream, with the lunch basket floating ahead of him.

Andrewshek stood in the middle of the stream, crying.

Auntie Katushka picked up her umbrella with the long crooked handle. Auntie Katushka ran along the shore

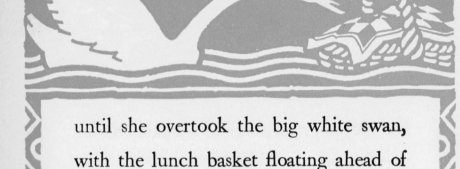

until she overtook the big white swan, with the lunch basket floating ahead of him.

She caught the handle of the picnic basket in the crook of her long handled umbrella. She drew the basket safely to shore.

"Well! well!" said Auntie Katush-ka, as she spread the red and white nap-

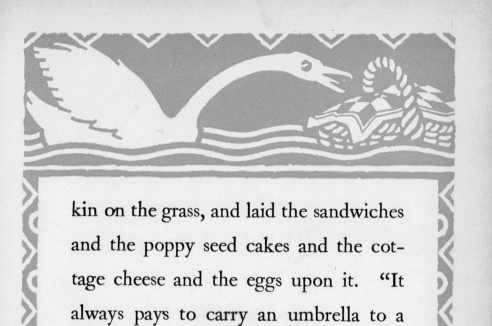

kin on the grass, and laid the sandwiches and the poppy seed cakes and the cottage cheese and the eggs upon it. "It always pays to carry an umbrella to a picnic."

ERMINKA AND THE RED TOPPED BOOTS

ONCE upon a time there was a little girl and her name was Erminka. When Erminka was exactly four and one half years old, her Uncle

Anton came to her house from the old country. Erminka's brother was one year and two days younger than Erminka and much smaller.

Erminka's Uncle Anton brought a set of wooden dolls for Erminka from the old country. Erminka liked the wooden dolls, although she did not like most dolls very much. The dolls' blue dresses

were painted on; the dolls' pink arms were painted on; the dolls' red shoes were painted on.

Uncle Anton brought Erminka's brother a pair of red topped boots. Uncle Anton had bought the red topped boots from a shoemaker in the old country. "I will take a large pair of red topped boots," he said to the shoemaker.

ERMINKA LIKED THE WOODEN DOLLS

"It is better to have the boots too large than too small. If they do not fit now, they will in a year. Little boys grow very fast."

The red topped boots were too big.

"You will have to wait at least a year before you are large enough to wear them," Erminka's mother said.

"Oh, then the red topped boots will

be just right for me!" cried Erminka, "for I am just a year and two days older! May I wear them?"

The red topped boots were too big for Erminka.

"I can wear three pairs of thick stockings with the red topped boots, Mother," she said, "and then they will fit me."

In the morning Erminka did not bother to find three pairs of thick winter stockings. She put on her thin white socks and slipped the boots on over them quickly.

After breakfast Erminka's mother went into the garden at the back of their house to pick butter beans and tomatoes. Erminka went along to carry the basket.

She wore the red topped boots.

"I must show my red topped boots to those tomato plants at the end of the garden," Erminka said to her mother. "The red tomatoes and the red tops on my boots are just the same color."

She ran down the path in a great hurry.

"See!" she called to the tomato

"MY RED–TOPPED BOOTS AND YOUR RED TOMATOES ARE THE
SAME COLOR"

plants. "My red topped boots and your red tomatoes are the same color! Aren't they beautiful?"

Just then Erminka and her red topped boots slipped. Erminka found herself flat upon her back and flat upon her favorite cucumber vine.

"Oh dear! oh dear! you have crushed a cucumber, Erminka!" cried the tomato

ERMINKA HAD DONE MORE THAN CRUSH ONE CUCUMBER

plants.   "Oh dear! oh dear!"

But Erminka had done more than crush one cucumber.   She had sat upon ten cucumbers and two juicy red tomatoes and one little bean vine and two fat summer squashes.

In the evening after supper Erminka's mother said to Erminka's father, "What

do you think Erminka did to-day in the garden?"

"I do not know," said Erminka's father as he puffed on his long pipe. "Had it something to do with the red topped boots?"

"Yes!" said Erminka and her mother at the same time. "How did you guess so quickly?"

ERMINKA AND THE
CRATE OF CHICKENS

RMINKA, I need eighteen duck eggs. I think I shall go to market

for them," said Erminka's mother.

"May I go with you? May I carry the little basket? And may I carry some eggs? And oh, Mother!" said Erminka, "may I wear the red topped boots?"

"Will you be very careful, Erminka, and not upset anything to-day, if you wear the red topped boots?"

"I will be careful, Mother, if I may

wear my red topped boots," said Erminka. "I look so beautiful in my nice
red topped boots."

"Your brother's red topped boots,"
reminded Erminka's mother.

"Well, Erminka," said Erminka's
mother, as she locked the kitchen door.
"I am ready to go to market now. I

think I will buy some gooseberries, too. Then we can have gooseberry tarts."

"May I make some tarts, too, and have a tea-party?" Erminka asked.

".Yes, indeed!" said her mother.

Erminka and her mother started for the market. They went down a hill and across the tracks and up two blocks until they came to a big red shed.

ERMINKA AND HER MOTHER STARTED FOR THE MARKET

It was the market. Inside, the farmers and the farmers' wives were selling vegetables and fruit and chickens and flowers and one farmer had five little white pigs for sale.

Erminka's mother saw many friends among the farmers' wives.

"How do you do, Mrs. Smith?" she would say. "Have you any sweet

butter this morning?"

"How do you do, Mrs. Gray? Have you any nice fresh buttermilk?"

"Good morning, Mrs. Popolovski! Have you any nice little cabbages to-day?"

Erminka grew tired of visiting with all these friends. She wandered off by herself.

She saw a crate full of chickens. "You nice chickens!" she said. "Wouldn't you like to see my red topped boots?"

"Yes, indeed!" said the chickens.

Erminka opened the door of the crate with the toe of her red topped boot.

As soon as the crate was open, five white chickens flew past Erminka. The market was upset. Everyone stopped

FIVE WHITE CHICKENS FLEW PAST ERMINKA

buying apples and selling eggs and ran after the chickens.

The chickens flew wildly about the market in all directions. One chicken fluttered out of the front door of the market and down the street. Only a baby chicken was left in the crate.

The market master and the farmers caught the chickens and put them back

in the crate.

"I did not mean to let the chickens run away, Mother," said Erminka. "But it looked so easy to open the door of the crate with the toe of my red topped boot."

"Your brother's red topped boot," reminded Erminka's mother.

In the evening after supper Erminka's

mother said to Erminka's father, "what do you think Erminka did to-day at the market?"

"I do not know," said Erminka's father, as he puffed on his long pipe. "Had it something to do with the red topped boots?"

"Yes!" said Erminka and her mother at the same time. "How did you guess so quickly?"

"HAD IT SOMETHING TO DO WITH THE RED–TOPPED BOOTS?"

ERMINKA AND THE
DUCK POND

I THINK we shall have to go to the
shoestore and buy Erminka a pair
of pretty black slippers," said Erminka's

mother. "Perhaps then she will not go poking her toes into places where they do not belong."

"That is a fine idea," said Erminka's father.

The next afternoon Erminka and her mother set off for the shoestore to look for a pair of pretty black slippers. On the way they stopped to pay a visit.

The house of Erminka's mother's friend was in a garden full of fruit trees and sweet smelling flowers.

"Let us go and sit in the garden," said Erminka's mother's friend.

They went into the garden and sat down on a white bench under an apple tree. Soon they began to talk very fast about friends in the old country.

Erminka grew tired of visiting. She ran down to the end of the garden to see the ducks.

Four brown ducks with yellow bills and one large white duck were swimming in a little duck pond at the end of the garden. The ducks swam lazily around and around, until they saw Erminka and her red topped boots.

FOUR BROWN DUCKS WITH YELLOW BILLS AND ONE LARGE WHITE
DUCK WERE SWIMMING

"Would you like to see my red top-ped boots?" called Erminka.

The ducks came up to the shore. They pecked at Erminka's boots with their long bills. One big duck came up on the shore beside Erminka.

Erminka was afraid of ducks when they came so close and pecked. Er-minka took three steps backward, away from the duck pond.

The edge of the duck pond was very muddy. Erminka slipped. She sat down with a bump in the soft mud. The little ducks paddled away to the other end of the little pond when they heard the splash. The muddy water splattered on the white feathers of the big duck. He waddled back to the pond. He was

THE MUDDY WATER SPLATTERED ON THE WHITE FEATHERS OF
THE BIG DUCK

very angry.

Erminka's red topped boots were drenched with mud.

In the evening after supper Erminka's mother said to Erminka's father, "What do you think Erminka did today?"

"I think I can guess," said Erminka's

father, as he puffed on his long pipe. "I guess that Erminka bought a pair of pretty black slippers."

"No, indeed!" said Erminka and her mother at the same time.

Erminka went to the cupboard and brought out the sad-looking red topped boots.

"I fell in the duck pond," she said.

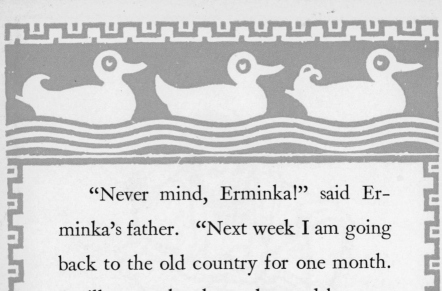

"Never mind, Erminka!" said Erminka's father. "Next week I am going back to the old country for one month. I will go to the shoemaker and buy another pair of red topped boots that will be just your size."

THE SHOEMAKER IN THE OLD COUNTRY

THROUGH THE FENCE

ERMINKA and her mother and her little brother went to live at Erminka's uncle's house, while Erminka's father was in the old country. Ermin-

ON THE WAY TO THE UNCLE'S HOUSE

ka's uncle lived across the tracks and up a hill, in a yellow house with a dark red roof and a little garden. The house was next door to the little green house where Andrewshek lived. There was a high fence between the two gardens.

Erminka's uncle was a carpenter. He had made Erminka three little chairs and a little table and painted them a nice

bright blue.

One warm summer afternoon Erminka took her three little blue chairs
and her little blue table out into the garden.

"Now we will play tea-party," she
said to her little brother.

Erminka's little brother was such a
tiny boy that he did not play tea-party in

ERMINKA'S LITTLE BROTHER

the way Erminka wanted.

Erminka saw Andrewshek next door,
playing in his garden.

"Please come over and play tea-party
with my little brother and me!" Erminka
called to Andrewshek.

"How can I get over into your yard?
My Auntie Katushka has tied the gate
tight shut. I used to swing on the gate

so much that the kitten and the chickens would run out into the road."

"Here is a nice little hole in the fence," said Erminka. "Perhaps we can make the hole bigger, so you can crawl through."

Erminka and her little brother and Andrewshek all tugged at a board and shook it and pulled it as hard as they

could.

After a long time Andrewshek was able to crawl through the hole. Andrewshek sat down in the third little blue chair.

"Will you have a cup of tea, Andrewshek?" asked Erminka.

"Yes, thank you; I will have a cup of tea," said Andrewshek.

"YES, THANK YOU; I WILL HAVE A CUP OF TEA," SAID ANDREWSHEK

"Yes, thank you; I will have a cup of tea, too," said a voice behind Erminka.

It was the white goat. She had poked her way through the hole in the fence.

"Yes, thank you; I will have a cup of tea and some cakes, too," said a voice behind Andrewshek.

It was the dog. He had crawled

IT WAS THE WHITE GOAT

through the hole in the fence.

"Yes, thank you; we will have two cups of tea and some cakes, too," said two voices behind Erminka's little brother.

Two of Auntie Katushka's chickens had fluttered through the fence.

"Dear! dear! what shall we do?" said Erminka to Andrewshek. "We have

no more cups and no chairs for them to sit upon."

"We *could* sit on the table," said the white goat politely.

"But then there would be no room for the dishes and the cakes!" said Er-minka.

"I think I will be going home then," said the white goat.

"I think I will be going home then," said the dog.

"We think we will be going home then," said the chickens.

"I think I will be going home, too," said Andrewshek.

The white goat poked her way through the hole in the fence. The dog crawled through the opening and

the two chickens fluttered through after him.

Then Andrewshek crept through the fence.

Auntie Katushka was on the other side.

"What shall I do with a runaway goat, Andrewshek?" asked Auntie Katushka.

AUNTIE KATUSHKA WAS ON THE OTHER SIDE

"I would put him to bed," said Andrewshek.

"What shall I do with a runaway dog, Andrewshek?" asked Auntie Katushka.

"Put him straight to bed," said Andrewshek.

"What shall I do with two runaway chickens, Andrewshek?" asked Andrew-

shek's Auntie Katushka.

"Put them straight to bed," said Andrewshek.

"And what shall I do with a runaway little boy?" asked Auntie Katushka.

"I don't know," said Andrewshek.

"I do," said Auntie Katushka.

Then Andrewshek's Auntie Katushka picked Andrewshek up in her arms

and carried him in to his fine feather
bed.

TO HIS FINE FEATHER BED

THE TEA PARTY

THE next morning Andrewshek's Auntie Katushka said to Andrewshek, "I think I will make some poppy seed cakes."

Then she took some butter and some
sugar and some flour and some milk and
nine eggs and rolled out some nice little
cakes.

"Why are you making so many nice
little poppy seed cakes?" asked Andrewshek.

"Because we are going to have a tea-
party this afternoon," said Auntie Ka-

tushka. She sprinkled each little cake with some of the poppy seeds she had brought from the old country.

"Who is coming to the tea-party?" asked Andrewshek, as he watched his Auntie Katushka put the poppy seed cakes in the oven.

"Erminka and Erminka's mother and Erminka's little brother," said

Auntie Katushka.

"Oh, goody!" said Andrewshek. "And I hope Erminka brings her wood- en dolls."

Andrewshek's Auntie Katushka took off her kitchen apron and hung it on a nail beside the door. She took the nice little cakes out of the oven and put them

SHE TOOK THE NICE LITTLE CAKES OUT OF THE OVEN

on the table to cool. Then she went to the cupboard drawer and took out her very best silk apron and the bright shawl which she had brought from the old country. She laid the apron and the shawl on the fine feather bed.

"When it is time for the tea-party, I will put these on," said Auntie Katushka to Andrewshek. "Now I am going next

door to invite Erminka and Erminka's mother and Erminka's little brother to the tea-party. Please watch the kitchen door while I am gone. Be sure that the kitten and the dog and the chickens do not come into the house."

"Yes, indeed! I will watch the kitchen door while you are gone next door," said Andrewshek. "And I will

be sure that the kitten and the dog and the chickens do not come into the house."

But all Andrewshek really did was to put on Auntie Katushka's very best silk apron and her bright shawl and walk back and forth and back and forth in front of the mirror. He paid no attention to the kitchen door.

BACK AND FORTH IN FRONT OF THE MIRROR

Just as Andrewshek was walking back and forth and back and forth in front of the mirror for the eleventh time, he heard a great commotion at the kitchen door. The kitten and the dog and the two chickens and the white goat had come into the kitchen.

They went straight to the kitchen table.

"Don't I see poppy seed cakes?" the white goat asked Andrewshek.

"They smell delicious!" said the kitten and the dog and the two chickens.

"Auntie Katushka made the poppy seed cakes for a tea-party," said Andrewshek.

"Are we invited to the tea-party?" asked the white goat.

"Are we invited to the tea-party?" asked the kitten and the dog and the two chickens.

"I think not," said Andrewshek. "Here comes Auntie Katushka, I will ask her."

The kitten and the dog and the two chickens and the white goat ran out of the door and into the garden as fast as

they could go. Andrewshek took off
the best silk apron and the bright shawl
and laid them on the fine feather bed.

"Erminka and Erminka's mother and
Erminka's little brother will come to our
tea-party at exactly half past three," said
Andrewshek's Auntie Katushka.

At exactly half past three Erminka

and Erminka's mother and Erminka's little brother came to the tea-party.

Erminka brought her wooden dolls. Erminka wore her new black slippers.

Erminka and Andrewshek and Erminka's little brother played together with Erminka's dolls around the corner of the house, near the front gate. Erminka said, "My mother says we may

have a tea-party for you and your Auntie
Katushka at my house to-morrow and
have gooseberry tarts."

"Goody!" said Andrewshek.

Andrewshek's Auntie Katushka
spread a clean white table cloth on the
table under the apple tree in the garden.
She brought out two plates of poppy

SHE SPREAD A CLEAN WHITE CLOTH ON THE TABLE

seed cakes and five cups and saucers and five spoons and five napkins. Then she went back into the house to get some strawberry jam.

The white goat and the kitten and the dog and the two chickens came and sat down on the bench beside the table under the apple tree in the garden. They sat very quiet with their hands

THEY SAT VERY QUIET WITH THEIR HANDS FOLDED

folded.

"If we behave nicely," said the white goat, "perhaps Andrewshek's Auntie Katushka will let us join the tea-party."

Andrewshek's Auntie Katushka came out on the porch with a bowl of strawberry jam in her hand. She saw the white goat and the kitten and the dog and the two chickens sitting quiet on the

bench, with their hands folded.

"Well! well!" said Auntie Katushka. "Some more friends have come to our tea-party. I hope they will like poppy seed cakes and strawberry jam, too."

And they did.